MW00446843

Cello

mel bay presents

The Student Cellist:
Bach

by Craig Duncan

Visit us on the Web at http://www.melbay.com — E-mail us at email@melbay.com

Contents

This collection includes both teaching compositions of J. S. Bach as well as easy arrangements of several of his most popular works. The pieces are all played in first position. The book begins with the easiest arrangements and progresses in level of difficulty. Most of the piano parts double the cello to aid in performance.

Menuet
from Anna Magdalena's Notebook

J. S. Bach

March
from Anna Magdalena's Notebook

J. S. Bach

Menuet

from Anna Magdalena's Notebook

J. S. Bach

Musette

from Anna Magdalena's Notebook

J. S. Bach

Bourrée
from French Suite Number 5 BMV 816

J. S. Bach

Gavotte
from French Suite Number 5 BWV 816

J. S. Bach

Gavotte

from Sixth Violoncello Solo Sonata

J. S. Bach

Bourrée I
from French Overture

J. S. Bach

Arioso

J. S. Bach

Jesu, Joy of Man's Desiring

Chorale from Cantata Number 147

J. S. Bach

12

Sheep May Safely Graze

from the Birthday Cantata

J. S. Bach

Fughetta

J. S. Bach

15 ritard

Great Music at Your Fingertips

mel bay presents

The Student Cellist:
Bach

by Craig Duncan

1 2 3 4 5 6 7 8 9 0

Visit us on the Web at http://www.melbay.com — E-mail us at email@melbay.com

Contents

This collection includes both teaching compositions of J. S. Bach as well as easy arrangements of several of his most popular works. The pieces are all played in first position. The book begins with the easiest arrangements and progresses in level of difficulty. Most of the piano parts double the cello to aid in performance.

Menuet

from Anna Magdalena's Notebook

J. S. Bach

March

from Anna Magdalena's Notebook

J. S. Bach

Menuet

from Anna Magdalena's Notebook

J. S. Bach

Musette

from Anna Magdalena's Notebook

J. S. Bach

Bourrée
from French Suite Number 5 BMV 816

J. S. Bach

Gavotte
from French Suite Number 5 BWV 816

J. S. Bach

Gavotte

from Sixth Violoncello Solo Sonata

J. S. Bach

Bourrée I
from French Overture

J. S. Bach

19

Arioso

J. S. Bach

Jesu, Joy of Man's Desiring

Chorale from Cantata Number 147

J. S. Bach

Sheep May Safely Graze

from the Birthday Cantata

J. S. Bach

Fughetta

J. S. Bach

Great Music at Your Fingertips